The pillars were made of porcelain.
The roof gleamed with real gold.

The palace garden bloomed
with rare flowers.

Tiny bells tinkled
in the breeze.

One day, the emperor was reading about his palace. He read:

The palace boasts many wonders...

the emperor smiled to himself

...but most wonderful of all is the song of the nightingale.

"WHAT?" snapped the emperor.
"I've never heard of this nightingale. Bring it here AT ONCE!"

Unfortunately, none of his ministers or servants
had heard of the nightingale either.

They combed
distant meadows.

They startled frogs out of ponds.

At last, in trees at the very edge of the garden,
they heard a soft, sweet sound...

It was a little brown bird.

"Are you the nightingale?" they asked.
"The emperor wants you to sing to him!"

My song sounds best among the trees,

said the nightingale.

But she flew to the palace and sang her sweet, soft song.

The emperor loved it so much, he begged her
to stay and sing to him every day.

The emperor gave the nightingale
a fancy golden cage
and fine silk ribbons.

"You shall have the best of
everything," he said.

He invited musicians to play alongside her...

...and scholars to write about her.

A while later, on the emperor's birthday, a gift arrived.

It was a clockwork
nightingale, glittering
with gold and jewels.

If you turned a key in its side,
it played a stiff, clockwork tune.

"How BEAUTIFUL!"
exclaimed the emperor. Dazzled,
he had eyes for nothing else.

The emperor played the clockwork nightingale
every day and **every** night.

He forgot all about the little brown bird.

Until one day, he turned the key to hear a sharp **TWANG** and then... nothing.

Some part of the clockwork had snapped.

No one knew how to fix it.

Now the emperor longed for the
little brown bird.

But she had long since flown away.

The servants searched
high and
low.

This time, no one could find her.

The emperor was heartbroken.

He took to his bed
and stayed there.

His room was full of silence and shadows.

His doctors feared he was close to death.

But then, a sweet, soft song drifted
through the open window...

...and the darkness started to lift.

The little brown bird had come back –
and the emperor began to get better.

"You are a true friend," he told her.
"Please, stay with me like before!"

Not in a cage, replied the bird.
But I will make my nest in
your garden and visit you often.

And she did.

The Emperor and the Nightingale is based on a story by Hans Christian Andersen. He lived in Denmark in the 19th century and wrote many famous fairytales.

Edited by Lesley Sims
Designed by Laura Nelson Norris

First published in 2019 by Usborne Publishing Ltd., Usborne House, 83-85 Saffron Hill,
London EC1N 8RT, England. www.usborne.com Copyright © 2019, 2018 Usborne Publishing Ltd.